T0124213

LIFE AND TIMES OF
APPLEBEE JONES

The Missing Crane
Book 2

BILLY MARTIN

authorHOUSE®

AuthorHouse™
1663 Liberty Drive
Bloomington, IN 47403
www.authorhouse.com
Phone: 1 (800) 839-8640

Published by AuthorHouse 06/02/2017

ISBN: 978-1-5246-9535-4 (sc)
ISBN: 978-1-5246-9534-7 (e)

Print information available on the last page.

1

L EROY DOBBS, A SAN FRANCISCO Journalist, was dressed and
hurrying down the stairs of the hotel. He wanted to get a fresh
start on the day. Eager to get to Miss Millie's boarding house and
sit with Reverend Jones. He was eager about writing the next chapter in
the life of Applebee Jones. He knew he had a great story and the editor/
publisher was encouraging him to gather all the material.

He stopped at the bakery and purchased another freshly baked apple
pie, Applebee's favorite. Wrapped in a cloth, he hurried across the street
with the aroma of the pie filling the air. He followed along the homes
until he reached Miss Millie's boarding house. He spotted her outside
near the front door trimming the potted plants that aligned the front of
the houses. She turned and saw him coming.

"Mr. Dobb, it's been several days since we saw you last, are you back
to see Reverend Jones again? She asked.

"Yes, I was able to complete our first interview and I needed a few
days to complete my notes." As he moved the hot pie from one hand to
the other. "Is the Reverend available? Dobbs asked as he moved up the
steps to the screen door.

"He's right where you left him the last time you were here. And that
apple pie smells fantastic. You know what that means don't you Mr.
Dobbs? She replied as she turned to continue trimming her prized rose
bush.

"I will leave you a large piece, I remember Miss Millie." Dobbs
replied back.

Dobbs opened the screen door and walked through the entrance
way into the parlor. This time he was careful not to let the screen door

slam shut. As it closed he could hear Miss Millie shout. "Thank you Mr. Dobbs."

Applebee sat quietly in his wheel chair in front of the window as he did the last time he visited him.

"Hello Reverend Jones, it's me Leroy Dobbs. I brought another apple pie for you to enjoy, it's fresh, just came out of the oven."

Applebee moved the wheelchair around so that he could face Dobbs. He could smell the aroma of the apple pie which made his white eye brows rise.

"Don't just hold it boy, set it down. And keep it covered I want a chuck of pie later and I don't want any bugs having their way with it. He remarked.

Dobbs set the pie down on the table closest to Applebee's chair and made sure the cloth covering it was in place.

"I was hoping that we could talk some more today. I completed the story you told me and sent it off." Dobbs stated as he pulled out a tablet and some pencils.

"We can do that." Applebee replied back. "What do you want to know? And let's not spend too much time on it, I don't want that pie to get cold and old lady Harper to get wind of the pie. She can smell out things a mile away."

"What happened after the events that took place? After you faced the Connelly boys? Dobbs asked.

Applebee grunted and smiled. "You know things were much quieter in town after that. I decided to let things calm themselves down in town. I still needed to do some planning on the bank, but with everything that had happened, the town had finally come alive. I was getting the hang of the preacher business and we were starting to get busy. I was learning a lot from AJ. Without him I would probably have gotten myself in a lot of trouble. AJ and Moon had figured out a way to keep Donk inside the coral and secure him inside the stable, that darn mull. We added a new member to the group, a rat killer, Mr. Sterling Price was his name, and he was busy doing his job, catching rats."

"So tell me what happened next? Dobbs asked.

"Well, let me see" wheeling his wheelchair around to face the window.

2

T HE MORNING WAS CRISP AND the smell of rain was in the air. The dark clouds hung over the town as the rising sun tried to break through the cracks of the clouds. The town was quiet with only a few individuals moving about. Mostly those that were trying to find their way home from a night of drinking and gambling and a few who didn't seem to know where they were going or what they were doing.

A supply wagon could be heard moving through the center of town being pulled by a team of two large horses as its wooden wheels cut through the soft soil until it could be heard only in the distance as it made its way out of town.

Moon stretched his arms, stood up and walked out of the stable area where he and AJ had their rooms. He rolled a cigarette as usual, lite it and leaned against the side of the stable door puffing out cloud of raw smoke which lifted into the air.

It was quiet and calm that morning. The events of the past weeks were very eventful and Moon felt confident that the problems that had plagued the town were now finally over. At least that what he hoped. The Connelly brothers were now gone and their ranch hands were now under control. He and AJ had played a big role in helping settling the town's issues and now he needed to help Applebee Jones make his way through the churches business. Moon was unsettled with the way Applebee handled himself as a minister of the town congregation. Applebee was so different in the way he presented himself, compared to the last pastor who was reluctant to get too involved in any of the towns business.

"This man packs a gun and isn't afraid to use it," Moon thought to himself as another cloud of smoke lifted into the air.

He suddenly heard the sound of something crashing against the walls inside the stable. He turned quickly and tossed the remaining cigarette on the ground as AJ walked out.

"What's going on in there? He asked AJ.

"You know that rat that's been eating holes in the grain bags?

"Yeah, what about it? He replied back.

"Well, here he is," as AJ raised up his arm from behind his back holding the rat by the tail. "He's not going to be doing that again."

"Get rid of that rat will you." Moon stated.

"You know what we need? AJ asked.

"What do we need? Moon replied

"We need a rat killer. A big fat cat. One that likes to hunt down rats." AJ stated as he walked away with the rat.

"Now where are we going, to get a rat killing cat? Moon asked. "Besides the cat will probably spook the horses and Donk."

"Would you rather have rats eating the grain maybe making a nest in your bunk? AJ replied back, "Besides I know where we can get a mean, nasty rat killer. Old man Todd, the man who runs the meat shop. He's got cats all over the place." AJ stated. "I'm sure he won't miss one cat."

"Make sure it's a male cat. We don't need a wagon full of cats if you get the wrong cat." Moon replied. "I remember when my brother brought home a cat, when we were young. I can't remember where he found it, but he raised it took good care of it and it was fun having it around. He would put a bucket over the cat and we would watch that bucket move all over the place. Mom caught us and made us each wear the bucket." Moon and AJ laughed. "But soon we found out it was a female cat and it had kittens and before you know it we had cats all over the place. They're like rabbits, one day you got one, the next day you got a dozen."

The morning sun finally broke through the clouds and began to warm the morning air. The town was now becoming busy as freight wagons began rolling into town. Applebee walked out the back door and made his way to the stable where AJ and Moon were busy feeding the horses.

"What's this note that was laying on the table this morning? Applebee asked.

"Mr. Granger stopped by this morning and left it. I thought you were still sleeping so I put it on the table." AJ stated as he tossed more hay into the horse's stall.

"What's he wants? Applebee asked.

"It seems that's Mrs. Crane passed away two days ago and the remaining relative wants to have a church service for her." AJ replied back as he laid the pitch fork against the wall. "He said she's already in a box and ready to go."

"Ready to go, go where? Applebee asked.

"In the ground." AJ replied looking at Moon with a surprised look.

"You mean we got to do that again? Applebee replied back as he sat down on several stacks of grain.

"Well, Reverend you know you are the only preacher in town." Moon stated.

"Yeah, I know that. What happened to the days when you just dug a hole and tossed them in, and that was that?

"You're not on the prairie anymore Reverend," Moon stated as AJ laughed. "Dig a hole and toss them in."

"Sometimes Reverend I think you got none of that religious training at all." Moon remarked. "Didn't you go to some school?

"Yeah, of course," Applebee thought for a second, "I wasn't at the top of my class. More like the bottom of the class." Applebee stated hoping that would satisfy Moons question.

"You want me to organize the service? AJ asked.

"Of course, you put the details together and let me know. I've got business in town this morning. But don't make it too long. I don't like long goodbyes."

3

AFTER SOME COFFEE AND SEVERAL of Moons homemade biscuits, Applebee walked the short distance into the town. He was greeted along the way by the town's people and tipped his hat to them as they passed. He felt comfortable with his appearance now and cleaning up the cities bullies made him kind of a hero to most. He could see the Sheriff's office in the distance as the two deputies were sitting outside with their chairs leaning against the office outer wall. As he came closer the deputies noticed him and sat up straight in the chairs and tipped their hats.

"Morning boys," Applebee stated as he passed by. "Are you keeping the peace today?

They said nothing just nodded as he went by. Watching him continue on his way. Applebee slowed down and took a close look at the bank across the street. There were several people inside and several wagons outside. He had some idea of the schedule that the bank operated on but wasn't clear on the inside since he had only been inside once.

He decided to cross the street and enter the bank and change some bills that he had into smaller ones, this would be his change to see the layout of the bank once more.

As he walked in, he was noticed by those inside and they greeted him with much flare. They shook his hand and the ladies fussed over him. He smiled and didn't say much as he was not familiar with what to say or answer any questions without AJ being with him. So he smiled, nodded and presented himself the best he could. He was moved to the front of the line by the ladies and faced the bank clerk. He handed him some paper money and asked if he could be given smaller bills. The clerk was excited to meet the Reverend and quickly made the change that he asked for. Applebee looked around the room and noticed behind the clerk is where the vault was located. The door was unlocked and partially open. Behind the counter where several desks with clerks doing something and to the very back was a solid metal door that appeared to be opened only from inside the bank. A metal cage surround the counter space extended to the ceiling with only a small opening for the clerks to operate from.

"This would not be easy." Applebee thought to himself. "This place had more to it than I thought for such a small town. This will need some good planning."

Just as Applebee was about to leave, AJ hurried in. He pulled Applebee to the side.

"Mr. Granger is waiting for you; he wants to talk to you." AJ stated.

"Who's Mr. Granger?

"He's the man who left the note, you know, about Mrs. Crane and the funeral service for her. I guess he didn't want to spend time with me, only you." AJ stated. "He has some other man with him. It looks kind of official."

"Okay, I'll be there in a minute." Applebee tucked the bills into his vest pocket. AJ ran back to the church to inform them that he was on his way.

Applebee soon returned and rounded the corner to the back of the church where the two men were standing. Granger was a small man in his fifties. Gray hair flared out from under his hat and his black suit coat appeared to be new. Next to him stood another man who carried a leather folder under his arm. He was much younger and stood tall and lean compared to Granger.

"I understand that you wanted to speak to me? Applebee stated.

"Yes sir. I'm Howard Granger and this is my attorney at law Mr. Taylor Tomkins. I wanted to speak to you concerning the death of Mrs. Crane, I'm sure that you heard that she had passed away several days ago, bless her little heart."

"Okay," Applebee stated. "What about her?

Moon and AJ looked at one another.

"I'm her last living relative and I wanted to have a small service for her in the next two days. It's only fitting, she was a very kind and generous person to us all, bless her little heart." Granger stated.

"So, make the arrangement with AJ," Applebee stated.

"This boy? Granger questioned.

"Yep, he handles all the affairs here and makes all the arrangements. He's my business partner of sorts." Applebee stated. "You don't have a problem with that do you?

"Oh, oh no, there's no problem, I'll have my attorney make all the arrangements with this young man. We'll see that the church is well taken care of for its efforts."

"Good." Applebee replied back as the two men walk away.

"I think there's something spooky about that man. I didn't know Mrs. Crane that well, but I didn't know she had any relatives here in town." Moon stated was he walked over and rolled another smoke. "She was a widower for some time and lived alone. Never saw that Granger man before. I wonder where he came from.

"What's that over there? Applebee asked.

"Where? AJ asked.

"Over there." Applebee stated.

"Oh, that's our rat killer." AJ replied back

"Rat killer?

"The stables have rats and we need something to catch the rats. There eating the grain." AJ explained.

"Where did you get the cat? He asked.

"From old man Todd, the butcher. He's got cats all over the place. He said I could have my choice of any of the cats he had. He has so many." AJ explained.

"Did you make sure it's a male cat? Applebee asked.

"Now you see. I made that same request. Make sure it's a male or we'll end up with a wagon load of cats just like Mr. Todd has." Moon stated.

"It's a male all right." AJ stated. "I checked."

"Okay. We need a name for him. Let's call him Mr. Sterling Price." Moon stated.

"Who's that? AJ asked.

"He was a military leader I think. I read that name somewhere. Seems like a good name for a rat killer." Moon replied.

"Is there any coffee left? Applebee asked.

"The pots on the stove as we speak, I just made a fresh pot while you were gone." Moon stated. "You know. I've been thinking about that Crane lady."

"What about her." Applebee asked as they started to walk toward the building.

"I just can't remember her ever having a relative at all. It seems that she had a child back east I think it was a boy. If I remember how the story goes. I don't think she had any living relatives around these parts." Moon stated.

"Maybe he lived somewhere else." AJ stated as the three walked into the building.

"Maybe, it just seems funny that this guy just now appears." Moon replied as he took a cloth and grabbed the coffee pot off the iron stove and poured Applebee some coffee.

"Look at that, our killer cat is already at work." AJ stated as they watched Mr. Sterling Price pass by the door, dragging a large rat.

"That was quick." Moon stated as he leaned out the door and watched the cat drag the rat away.

"What are we doing today? Applebee asked as he took a sip of the coffee.

"Nothing today." AJ replied back.

"Good, today would be a good day to go fishing." Applebee stated. "I noticed some fishing poles in the corner of the stable. What say you if we make it a day of it."

"Now that's what I like to hear." Moon stated with a large smile on his face. "And I know just the place to go."

They finished and gathered the items they needed and loaded the wagon. Moon hitched up the wagon.

"What about Mr. Granger and Mrs. Crane? AJ asked as he climbed into the wagon.

"Mrs. Crane is died isn't she? Applebee stated. "One more day isn't going to make much of a difference. Besides if we don't get any bites will come back. When we get to the meat shop, run in and get us some slices of that pressed meat I saw the other day. Moon you get some bread and cheese from the bakery shop. This should pay for it." Applebee stated as he handed each some cash.

The wagon moved out into the main street and rolled through town until it reached the meat shop. AJ jumped down and ran into the shop as Moon climbed down and walked to the bakery shop.

"Where you headed Preacher? A couple asked coming from another direction.

"We're going fishing today. Seems like a good day for fishing and it's been a while since I took some time off." Applebee replied back.

"The Potters fishing hole just outside of town is a good place to catch fish." The man stated. "I caught many a good size catfish there."

Moon returned as did AJ, each carrying their purchases. AJ placed everything into a leather bag as the wagon began to roll away passing the shops and saloons along the way. People tipped their hats while others waved.

"Seems like you're a popular person in this town now Reverend since them Connelly boys are not here anymore bothering people." Moon stated as the wagon passed the last building and made its way out into the country landscape.

"The sky sure cleared itself up, no rain today." Applebee stated. "What's the story on the Potters fishing hole?

"Where did you hear that name? Moon asked.

"That couple back there mentioned it when I told them we were going fishing." Applebee replied.

"Well, long ago there was a man named Potter. He lived just outside of town next to the river's edge. He had an old shack that he lived in. He used to work for some company that used to cut through the mountains for the railroad. He did the blasting. The story goes that he was always trying to develop some new kind of formula for the explosive powder. One day he had an accident and the powder exploded on him, the shack, and large area where the shack was sitting. They said you could hear the blast for miles. They never found him. The river filled in and now it's one of the best fishing spots there is. That's where we're headed to.? Moon asked.

As the wagon got closer to the river, the sound of the water could be heard as it rolled over the rocks. A large area of trees and growth lined the backs. They followed the river's edge and then stopped at a clearing.

"This is the place. Potter hole." Moon stated.

They climbed down from the wagon, gathered their items and follow Moon. They walked just a few feet to an area that was cut away from the river. Trees and large boulders covered the edge of the river. They found a small clearing that reached the river.

"This looks like a good spot." Moon stated.

"I can see where this must have been where the cabin was located." Applebee stated as he set up his pole and dug around the edge of the river for some worms.

"They say there's a fish in this water that is big as AJ, and no one's ever caught him. He's some smart fish." Moon stated as he set the worm on his hook.

"That's a mighty big fish." Applebee replied back.

"He's a big one, and he's smart too." Moon answered back as he tossed his line onto the water.

"Stand back everyone because I'm getting ready to catch that fish and I need some room to do it." AJ shouted out.

The river water ran slowly past them and small insects could be seen skipping off the top of the water. There was no breeze and the sun was warming the air. Applebee sat on a small flat rock and leaned back against another. Moon was sitting some 10 feet away from Applebee and AJ was next to the trees that hung over the river bank.

"Now this is the way to spend the day." Moon stated.

"You go fishing much? Moon asked Applebee.

"Not much now. When I was a kid, my brothers and I used to fish all the time. We would sneak away from the house and go down to the lake and spend all day fishing and more time swimming. Pa would finally figure out where we were and he'd come down there and haul us all back. It might have been different if we had caught some fish." Applebee explained.

"How about you Moon? AJ asked.

"I think I was the greatest fisherman there was. I used to catch fish, my bag was filled with fish. We used to use a cheese ball and toss that thing out there and those fish would fight over it." Moon stated.

"A cheese ball? AJ asked.

"Yep, a cheese ball." He replied.

Time had passed without any bits as they tossed stories around when suddenly AJ's pole all most bent in half. AJ grabbed his pole before it flew into the water. He pulled back on the pole to set the hook and felt the weight of the fish on his line. He looked over at Moon who was rolling a cigarette and Applebee who was leaning back with his eyes closed. AJ continued to pull on the pole and could feel the weight of the fish on the line. He knew he had caught a good size fish but would probably need some help. He held on tightly to the pole pulling and tugging.

"Moon," AJ stated.

"What," Moon replied back as he leaned back against the rock puffing away. Smoke lifting up above him.

"I'm going to catch the big one." AJ stated as he continued to pull and tug at his pole.

"Good, that will make us some good eating tonight." Moon replied back.

"I think I'll need some help." AJ replied back

"Maybe so, they say he's a big one. Been living in these water for some time. Never been caught. Smart fish." Moon replied back

"No I mean I need some help." AJ stated.

"When you get to that point, just let me know." Moon stated back as he continued puffing away.

"Moon," AJ shouted out, "I need some help."

Moon glanced over and saw AJ laying on the ground holding on to the pole. The pole was almost breaking in half. The line was moving violently from side to side. Moon jumped up and toss the cigarette and shouted to Applebee. Applebee looked over in surprise and saw what was going on and pulled his line out of the water and hurried over to where AJ was at.

"Hang on to that pole boy, don't let it go." Moon shouted out as Moon grabbed AJ who was just about in the water and pulled him onto the rock.

"Reverend, try to grab that line if you can, this boy done caught him the big one." Moon stated.

Applebee reached down to the water's edge and grabbed the line. He could feel the weight of the fish on the line. As he pulled on the line the line moved to his right and its weight was enough to pull Applebee off the rock he was standing on and into the water.

Moon stood AJ up, "Hold on tight, don't let go, I got to get the Reverend out of the water." Moon stated as he hurried over to the water's edge, grabbed Applebee who was still holding on to the line and pulled him out of the water.

"Come on Reverend," Moon stated.

"Let's try to work together," Moon shouted out as the three worked to pull the line. "This is the biggest fish I've ever seen."

With the end of the line reaching the surface, they could see the outline of the fish. And it was the big one. They maneuvered the line from one side to the other. AJ got tangled on the rocks, slipped and fell off the rock into the weeds and mud next to the rock.

"You okay? Moon asked.

"I'm okay," AJ replied back. "You got him yet?

"Reverend, get him close enough to the surface and I will reach down there and grab him and pull him up." Mood stated as Applebee pulled and tugged at the line as the big fish continued its battle.

With the fish at the surface, Moon leaned over the rock and reached down and grabbed the monster fish and tried to pull him out of the water. Applebee grabbed Moon by the legs and held on to him as the battle raged on. With one last tug, Applebee pulled on Moon and Moon held tight to the fish as the fish came out of the water. Still fighting, Moon pulled the fish away from the water. AJ climbed back on top of the rock and saw the size of the fish he had caught.

"Now that's a fish." Moon stated. "That's the biggest catfish I've ever seen. It must weigh all of fifteen to eighteen pounds."

"Maybe twenty pounds." AJ replied back as he wiped away the mud from his clothes.

"That's the biggest fish I've ever seen." Applebee stated as he kept his foot on the fish to keep him from falling back into the water.

The catfish rolled and twisted trying to regain its position and save itself. Applebee kept his large boot on its back and then reached into his coat and pulled out his pistol and pointed it at the catfish.

"What are you going to do with that? AJ asked.

"I'm going to stop it from moving around."

"You're going to blow a hole in it the size of my arm, and we'll lose a large section of the fish." AJ shouted back.

"Here, let me run this rope through it gills and we'll put him in the water to keep him fresh." Moon stated as he inserted the rope through the mouth and then through the gills. He pulled the large catfish over the rocks and let it fall into the water, then tied the rope to a small tree.

"That's enough fishing for me." Applebee stated. "I'm wet and I'm tired and the day has just begun. Let's gather our stuff and head back. "How come you're all muddy?

"I slipped on the rocks and fell into the muddy bank." AJ stated as he continued to wipe away the mud from his clothes. His hair was caked with mud and small twigs from the weeds.

They gathered their items and began loading them into the wagon. Moon returned and pulled the catfish out of the water and carried it to the wagon and laid it in the back with AJ.

"You got yourself a real fish story to tell now." Moon stated as he stepped back and watch the catfish as it again struggled. "Yep, got yourself a real fish story."

CHAPTER

4

As the wagon moved along the trail back toward town, AJ bounced around in the back of the wagon. They ate along the way. Each had a piece of the dried meat and baked bread that they had purchased before leaving town.

"What's that up there? Applebee asked as they came upon a fully saddled horse grazing alongside the road. Moon slowed the wagon down and then stopped just a few feet away from the grazing horse. Applebee jumped down from the wagon and cautiously approached the horse trying not to spook it. He grabbed the reins as the horse jolted at first, then settled down. Moon and AJ joined him.

"Look around, see if you can see anyone," Applebee stated as he looked at the horse for any injuries. Moon and AJ walked around the area but saw nothing. The grassy areas were thick and it took several minutes to wade through the tall grasses.

"He must be a run away." Moon stated. "There's no one around in any direction."

"He's been here a while. It's not sweaty. Everything is in tack and the horse has no injuries that I can see. Tie him to the back of the wagon. We'll take him into town with us. Someone will be looking for his horse." Applebee stated as Moon led the horse to the back of the wagon.

The wagon continued back to town with the mystery horse following behind. Applebee would peer over the landscape trying to see if there were was anyone on foot. But there was no movement in any directions.

They reached the outskirts of the town and slowly made their way along the street. Those passing by tipped their hats and some even waved. The business was operating and the street were crowded with cowhands and freight wagons.

"Did you catch anything? A man shouted from the front of the hardware store.

That excited AJ as he reached back and lifted up the catch with a proud smile on his face pointing to himself as the victor. It took several minutes for them to move through the street. Applebee peered over to the bank as they passed. It was busy as usual. Moon pulled the wagon over to the side of the street next to the Sheriff's Office. The two deputies were sitting outside the office when the wagon approached then stopped.

"I got something for you." Applebee stated as he jumped down from the wagon and walked to the back.

The two deputies sat up in the chairs and stood up and walked over to the wagon.

"What you got there Reverend? The one asked as they watched the horse being tied to the rail.

"Never seen that horse before, I wonder what happened to the rider? We'll take it to the stable and leave it there." Deputy stated as he reached over and took the reins and began to lead the horse to the stable. Applebee climbed up on the wagon.

"If no one claims him, I want him." Applebee stated. "And no funny business either you got that."

The wagon continued on until it reached the church as Moon directed it to the barn. AJ carried his prize inside and laid it on the table as the rat killer followed behind him.

"AJ," shouted Moon. "You unhitch the horse and I'll clean that monster fish you caught. We'll have fish tonight for dinner and get that rat killer out of the house. His job is out there not in here."

AJ chased Sterling Price out of the house and closed the door behind him. Sterling, as old as he was, slowly moved back to the long wooden bench, jumped up and took that position again. He used his large front paw to begin grooming himself stroking his faded yellow fur.

"I don't know why Sterling Price can't come in here, he's a part of this family now and does a great job in catching rats. He catches 2 to 3 a day. I vote that he gets to come inside."

"Vote," Moon states. "Who said anything about taking a vote?

"Voting is the best way to make a decision." AJ replied back.

"Somebody said something about a vote? Applebee asked as he walked into the room while Moon was preparing the fish.

"Young AJ there wants to take a vote that will allow Mr. Sterling Price the right to enter the house." Moon explained.

"A vote? Applebee stated back. "Since when do we have votes?

"It's the best way to decide an outcome." AJ stated. "I read in the paper that voting will become the biggest event in the future. According to the paper's story, citizens will be voting on all kinds of things, not just elections. If you want something done in the town, the citizens will have the right to vote and make the decision. There's even the idea that each person will have to pay some kind of tax to help pay for different things."

"Really," replied Applebee. "Taxes you say."

"The future is about to change. Look at all the changes there are now. I'm telling you the world is changing and we need to get in line with it." AJ stated. "In other countries they are doing all kind of new things. I read about this ship that has no sails and travels under the ocean water only."

"What you mean no sails. They row under the water? Moon replied.

"No, they don't row under the water. There are no oars. It has some kind of engine that allows them to go under the water. And it can carry several people."

"How do they breathe inside something like that? Moon asked.

"I guess they have some piece of equipment that makes the air for you to breathe." AJ replied. "That's what I'd like to do. I want to see all that stuff."

"Well, it sounds like we better get ourselves in line, and I guess voting is what we need to start with. How do we do that? Applebee asked as he poured himself a cup of coffee from the kettle that was sitting on the iron stove.

"That's easy. Everyone in favor of allowing Sterling Price to come inside with us with the exception of dragging some rat in with him, raise your hand." AJ stated.

"That includes not dragging any rats into our room in the stable too." Moon stated.

"Agreed." AJ replied back.

"Now do I get to vote on that too? Applebee asked.

"Do you sleep in the stable? AJ replied asked.

"No."

"We have to account for some things." AJ remarked.

AJ looked around and saw that everyone had raised his hand up.

"See there, we've already taken our first step into the future." AJ stated with a smile on his face. "Sterling Price is now a full member of this house and can come in when he wants to."

"Next we will be voting on the horses and chickens." Moon replied back as he placed several logs into the iron stove."

He placed a large cast iron skillet on the burner. Took some fat from a tin container and let it sizzle in the iron pan. He reached over and took an egg and broke it into a bowl. He then grabbed the fish slab and dropped into the whipped egg, then took it out and dropped it into some flour rolling it around several times.

"What are you doing? Applebee asked in wonder as he watched Moon.

"I read this in this old cook book I found at the general store. No one wanted to buy it so he gave it to me." Moon stated as he placed the coated fish into the pan. It crackled and fried itself into a crusty slab. He flipped it over several times, looked at it, and placed it on a tin platter and repeated the process again and again until all the slabs of fish were cooked.

"Do we have any of those cooked biscuits from this morning? Applebee asked.

Moon reached into the large covered container and pulled out several remaining biscuits from the morning.

"There's plenty here." as he handed the platter of fish to Applebee. "A fish sandwich."

Each began to eat this new discovered cooking method that Moon had prepared and it appeared that everyone like it as the fish quickly disappeared along with the biscuits.

"Something new." Applebee stated. "This has been a day of discovery."

Just as they were finishing and celebrating their history making events, when they heard a knock at the door. AJ opened the door.

"It's that attorney man, Mr. Tomkins." AJ stated.

"Thank you young man," Tomkins replied as he took off his hat at the entrance of the door. "I wanted to get the arrangement completed now that you're back from your journey and I do have payment to you for presiding over the event."

"AJ handles all of the arrangements around here for that stuff so you can talk to him about it." Applebee stated as he got up from the table and poured himself another cup of coffee.

"That will be fine." Tomkins replied back. "We would like to have a small funeral so we can move on to other matters."

"Tell me something Mr. Tomkins, there was some talk about Old lady Crane, I mean Mrs. Crane and her family. The thought was that she didn't have any local family or family elsewhere as that goes." Applebee asked as he sat back down at the table.

"I'm not sure I understand your question Reverend." Tomkins replied back.

"It's a simple question Sir, just where did Howard Granger come from? Applebee asked.

"I have been the family attorney for many years and I can as- sure you that Mr. Granger is the last remaining member of her family. Now here is what we would like to have done." Tomkins states as he hands AJ a piece of paper with the funeral instructions written on it, and then hands AJ some cash.

"I believe that will cover the funeral. I've taken care of the burial with the undertaker already."

Suddenly Tomkins felt something on his leg. He looked down and then quickly moved. Mr. Sterling Price was rubbing against his leg with a very loud purring sound.

Thank you for your time." Tomkins stated as he turned and left.

"Something smell fishy to me Reverend and it's not what I just cooked." Moon states.

"Welcome Mr. Sterling Price, as you are now a fully-fledged, voted member of this elite family, come on in." Applebee stated as the large yellow cat slowly wondered in taking his time as he slowly moved throughout the room examining all the details.

"What do you know about Mrs. Crane? Applebee asked.

"Well let me see," Moon replied." She used to come to church and had been for some time. She's very quiet and pretty much keeps to herself. I've heard that she has quite a lot of money. Mr. Crane died some time ago and he left a large sum of money. That's about all I know about her. Some said they didn't have any children. Others said they thought they had heard that they had a son, and he was back east somewhere. She never had any family elsewhere that ever came to see her. You want me to ask around? Moon asked.

"No, don't do that." Applebee stated. "Let's just get this done."

Moon Looked over and saw that Mr. Price had found himself a place of his own. He was sprawled out on a small wooden bench. He was purring loudly and doing a little cleaning of his own.

"They said all they wanted was a grave side funeral. They want you to say a few words and that's about it." AJ stated. "You want me to right a few lines for you?

"Do what you do best lad. Make it simple," Applebee replied back. "I'm going to take a walk over to the Sheriffs and see what up with the horse we brought in."

Applebee walked along the buildings until he reached the Sheriff's Office. The two deputies who were outside were gone for the day and only one deputy remained inside. Applebee walked in and closed the door behind him. The closing of the door made the deputy jump up.

"Reverend you surprised me." The elderly deputy remarked as he adjusted his gun belt. "What can I do for you?

"What did you find out about the horse we brought in? Applebee asked as he peered over to the wanted posters that were tacked up on the wall.

"Nothing. The saddlebags had some clothes in them, but there was no other information on who the horse belonged. Nothing on the horse. The clothes are over there on the table if you want to look at them."

Applebee walked over to the table and reached down and picked up several of the items on the table. Stacked on the table were several items, one pair of trousers, a shirt, extra socks, and several books on engineering. He turned the pages of the book and then stopped. One page appeared to be torn out. As he continued to turn the pages, a small piece of paper was logged between two of the pages. He made sure the deputy didn't see him remove the small folded piece of paper. He took the folded piece of paper and put it into his coat pocket. He continued looking through the books and then placed them on the table.

"Let me know if you find out anything more." Applebee remarked as he turned and walked out.

He crossed the street and walked toward the bank. It was almost closing time and most of those who were doing business in the bank were finishing up and leaving. He slowed down as he walked by noticing any missed details he hadn't seen before. The large vault door was still slightly open and the elderly guard remained in the same chair he was in the last time he passed by. The metal back door was going to be a problem as it was thick and had a large cross piece locked into place. All the windows were barred and the front door was a wooden door with iron doors just inside that closed behind them.

"This place is tight." Applebee thought to himself. "It was well designed by someone who wanted to make sure that no one ever got in and nothing ever got out."

He continued to the church as night fall was closing in on the balance of the day. The last of the freight wagons had passed by and most of the cowhands had settled down in the saloons. He could hear the piano banging away in the nearby saloon as he crossed the street and reached the entry of the church. He could see Moon feeding the horses and Sterling Price moving about.

He entered the room of the church and sat down by the table. AJ was placing several logs into the iron stove to warm the room and heat up the coffee kettle.

"I wrote some words down for tomorrow funeral. Nothing fancy, just appropriate words for such a lady." AJ stated.

"I stopped by the Sheriff's Office and asked if they had any information on the horse we brought in. All they found was the clothes in the saddlebag and a few engineering books. I went through the books and found a page missing in one of the books and this folded piece of paper."

"What does it say? Moon asked as he entered the room.

"It looks like part of a letter. It's hand written." Applebee remarked as he looked over the words. "It's hard to make out, the writing is old and faded. Here you see if you can read any of this." Applebee stated as he handed it to AJ.

"Another thing," Applebee stated as he reached for a tin cup. "The clothes were not the type that are worn in this part of the country."

"What you mean? Moon asked.

"The shirt was light and had a lacy feeling to it." Applebee stated. "It think who ever owned that horse came a long way."

"Did you see the horse? Moon asked.

"No, why? Applebee replied back.

"Did anyone check the saddle? Moon asked. "Lots of times the initials of the owner of the saddle is underneath. Somewhere on the leather."

"Can you read that? Applebee asked as he looked over at AJ.

"I can make out a few of the words. Let me work on it."

"You work on it while Moon and I go to the blacksmiths shop. I want to check out that saddle." Applebee stated as he and Moon left for the stable. The walked across to the other side of the street and passed by several businesses until they reached the barber shop. Down the alley, the Blacksmith and Stable was behind the barber shop. It was a large wooden building with two double doors and a small coral off to the side. Several wagons, and tack items were scattered on the outside of the building.

"There's a light on inside." Applebee stated as they got closer to the building. "There's the horse."

"Elmo has a room inside." Moon replied as they reached the double doors. "Elmo," Shouted Moon. "Come and open these doors."

"Moon is that you? Elmo shouted back. "Just a minute, give me a chance to get there."

One half of the double doors opened enough to allow the two to enter. Both Applebee and Moon squeezed past Elmo and stopped.

"Reverend Jones, what brings you to my fine establishment? I've heard much about you. Is there something I can do for you? Elmo asked.

"Yes, I wanted to take a look at the saddle that was on the horse that I brought in today." Applebee explained.

"It's not for sale you know. I have to keep it here until the Sheriff tells me I can sell it."

"Has anyone come by asking about it? Moon asked.

"A matter a fact there was." Elmo replied back. "Some city slicker looking guy came by and asked about it. I thought he might ask if it was for sale but he just looked at it and then left. Never said a word, just left."

"Can we see the saddle? Applebee asked.

"Sure it's on the railing over there." Elmo stated as he pointed to the back wall. "It's not much of a saddle. I think it's one of those cheap ones you can get."

Applebee and Moon walked to the back wall where the saddle was located. Applebee lifted it off the railing and laid it on the ground and rolled it over.

"Just what are you looking for? Elmo asked.

"Some initials or a name." Moon replied. "The name of the person who owns the saddle."

"You not going to find it there." Elmo stated. "Lift up the small leather piece next to the horn."

Applebee rolled it over and lifted up the leather piece that was attached to the bottom of the horn. There burned into the leather were the initials MJC.

"This old saddle had a piece that was attached to the horn so the rope would rub on the leather and not on the horse." Elmo explained. "It's a homemade piece that was added by someone. Probably a cowhand. They don't do that anymore."

"There it is. You were right Moon. The initials were burnt into the leather. Applebee stated. "CJC."

"So now we need to find out who is CJC." Moon replied back as he helped Applebee place the saddle back on the railing.

Moon and Applebee returned to the church building and found AJ busy at work trying to read what was written on the small piece of paper Applebee had taken from the engineering books.

"What did you find out? Moon asked AJ.

"Well, this is a piece of a letter that was torn from the original. From what I can figure out, the sentences are incomplete because of the way it was torn out and the words are so faded. There are only a few words that I can ever read, but I do know the person it was written to have the first two letters of CJ. The rest I can't be sure of. I figured out some of the words. I think this says, "come and see me," but that's about all I can read."

"So we know that CJ is probably the name of the person who was on the horse and the saddle has the initials CJC burnt into it." Moon stated.

"So what was this guy doing riding out this way and then disappearing and leaving his horse out in the middle of know where. His clothes were not that of a person from here that's for sure, so he must have come from a long distance." Applebee stated.

"Maybe he came from the East and he was traveling here to see someone, based on what AJ could figure out and I bet you his last name was Crane." Moon stated.

"Crane, you mean this guy was related to Mrs. Crane? The lady we're going to bury tomorrow? AJ asked.

"I bet you she wrote to him and told him to come and see her, maybe because she was sick and he made the trip out here and was stopped by someone who didn't want him to arrive." Moon explained.

"So you think that this guy is related somehow to Mrs. Crane." AJ asked.

"I bet my next batch of biscuits on it." Moon replied back. "And I think that Graham and Tomkins had something to do with it. Neither one is from around here. We don't know anything about either one. There's a rat in the house."

"And you think that Graham and Tomkins are the rats? Applebee asked.

"No, there's a rat in the house," Moon stated as he pointed to Mr. Sterling Price as he walked by carrying a small rat in his mouth.

"See, aren't you glad that we voted making Mr. Price a member of the family? AJ stated.

"I've got to admit, he sure is doing his job." Applebee replied back as they watched him go out the door and disappear.

"Mr. Price and Donk seem to be getting along just fine." Moon stated. "He follows Donk around the coral during the day and Donk seems to like his presents. He hasn't gotten out once since Mr. Price has joined us."

CHAPTER

5

The Funeral

THE UNDERTAKER ARRIVED AND CLIMBED down from his Hurst and walked to the back of the church. Moon saw him coming and called out to AJ and told him to find Applebee. AJ ran into the building and found Applebee leaving his room. He carried with him his Bible and the message that AJ had prepared.

"Okay Reverend, were ready to head over to the cemetery. You ready? The undertaker asked.

"I'm ready. Let's get this over with." Applebee replied back. "Are there many people joining us?

"Just a few. I'm heading for the cemetery and you can follow behind with the others." The undertaker stated as he turned and left walking back to his Hurst.

Like most of the funerals, the Hurst was dressed with black feathers on each of its corners. The horse that pulled it also had a large grouping of black feathers. A casket was sitting inside on a red colored blanket. Applebee, AJ and Moon followed behind the Hurst as it made its way through town to the cemetery. Towns people stopped and watched the Hurst go by, some tipping their hats.

The casket was taken out of the Hurst and set into position at the grave site and the small group of individuals who were attending along with Graham and Tomkins stood around the grave site. Applebee walked to the front, with AJ and Moon standing off in the distance and stared at those attending.

"Take off your hats," Applebee stated, as he removed his hat and opened his Bible, looking for the paper that AJ had placed in it.

"We're here today to send Mrs. Crane on into the next world, one of joy and happiness." Applebee read as all of the on lookers listened and many of the women began to tear up. He continued reading what AJ had prepared and when he finished he read a small prayer that was prepared. He then thanked everyone for coming. Everyone started to leave and began the walk back to town. Graham and Tomkins were far ahead of the group. Applebee, AJ and Moon were the last to join in the walk back to town following the Hurst.

"Once again Reverend you out did yourself." Moon stated as the three walked together. Did you see who followed us to the cemetery?

"Who," Applebee asked in wonder. "Who followed us to the cemetery?

"He stood by your feet as you spoke." Moon stated. And he following behind us right now."

Applebee stopped and quickly turned to see who Moon was speaking about. There in the distance was Mr. Sterling Price. Slowly moving his way back to town.

"He followed us to the cemetery and was standing right next to you the entire time you were speaking." Moon stated as he and AJ began to laugh.

Applebee turned around and continued walking. "He has good taste."

The three began to laugh as they reached the outer limits of town. Graham and Tomkins had disappeared as did the balance of those attending. The Hurst moved through town and reached the Undertakers building and entered through the alley to the rear of the building.

"Where do you think Graham and Tomkins went? Asked Moon.

"Probably to count their money." Applebee stated. "I think we need to find out a little more about Mrs. Crane, Graham and Tomkins. You know what I'd like to have? Applebee stated.

"What's that? AJ asked

"Since were all dressed in our finest attire, I'd like to have a chunk of apple pie and chase it down with something cool. How about you? He asked.

"I'm always ready for some apple pie," AJ replied, as the three walked past by the church and continued on until they reached the Hotel. They entered the lobby and was noticed by the desk clerk who gave a quick nod. They found a table near the window and sat down as the waitress joined them.

"Okay, what brings the three of you in here this day dressed in your best Sunday meeting clothes? She asked.

"These aren't our best, these are our very best." AJ stated.

"We just buried Mrs. Crane and now we'd like to have a chunk of apple pie, two mugs of cold beer and one cup of cold buttermilk for the lad." Applebee stated. "That sound good to you two?"

Moon and AJ eagerly agreed with Applebee's thought, as the waitress left for the kitchen.

"What's that noise? Applebee asked. "It almost sounds like Mr. Price."

"It is Mr. Price. He followed us in here. He's sitting next to me in the empty chair." AJ explained.

"I guess if he's a part of the family now, he should be here." Applebee stated. "But no apple pie for him. Give him some of your crust to chew on."

Just as they heard a familiar voice. One that is difficult to forget.

"Hello Reverend, I. I. I saw you in here and I want t.t.t to stop by and say howdy to you, howdy Moon and AJ." Harold stated with his stuttering voice.

"Harold, now that you're here, did you ever meet the late Mrs. Crane? Applebee asked.

"You bet I did. When she bought supplies from Swayne's store, I used to deliver them to her. I even did odd j. j...j....jobs for her. Why?

"Did she have any relatives, like possibly a son? Applebee asked.

"You know I.... I.... I saw a picture on a desk one time when I was replacing some hinges for her. I think she said it was her son. He's back East somewhere and was going to school at the time. When they moved out here, he remained there so he could finish." Harold replied back. "That was some time ago. I got to go Reverend. Swayne doesn't like me to be late."

Harold walked out of the dining room, through the lobby and disappeared from sight. The three finished eating and left returning to the church with Sterling Price following behind. They spotted Granger and Tomkins riding by heading North out of town.

"I think we need to make a visit to the Crane home. Let just say were going to see if there is anything they need during this sad time." Applebee stated.

"You want me to hitch up the wagon or the buckboard? We're going to clean it today." Moon stated.

"Wait a minute. You mean we have a buckboard? He asked. As they stopped.

"Yeah, it was given to us some time ago." Moon replied back. "It in back of the barn."

"And we've been riding in that wagon with hard wooden seats all this time." Applebee asked. "Why didn't you say something about having a buckboard? Does it have padded seats?

"Yes sir, it has nice padded seats." Moon replied. "And I didn't say anything because you said hitch up the wagon, so that's what we did."

Applebee stood quiet for a few seconds, "Oh brother, come on Mr. Sterling Price." Applebee stated as he turned to Mr. Price, both continued walking toward

CHAPTER

6

OON PULLED THE BUCKBOARD TO the side of the building and sent AJ in to find Applebee. The three loaded into the buckboard and started in the direction of the Crane ranch, located just a mile out of town. The ranch was still functioning with several hundred head of cattle grazing on the pastures just located North of town when AJ shouted out. "Stop."

Moon pulled back on the reins and stopped the buckboard and both he and Applebee turned around and looked at AJ.

"What's the matter? Applebee asked.

"Look." AJ replied pointing as the three were looking behind the buckboard as Mr. Sterling Price was following them at a full run.

"Well, it appears we forgot one." Moon stated as Mr. Price caught up to the buckboard and jumped in, sitting next to AJ.

"Let's go. Tell me something AJ, how come you picked Mr. Price? Applebee asked as the wagon continued on.

"He was the only one I could catch." AJ replied back.

Just off the main road was the entrance to the Crane house. A white fence surrounded the home with a large archway with the name Crane centered at the top. Standing next to the entrance was a large man holding a rifle. He stepped forward as the buckboard reached the archway.

"That's far enough." He shouted out. "What's your business here?

"We came here to see if there was anything we could do since we buried Mrs. Crane today. I'm Reverend Jones and this is Moon and AJ." Applebee stated.

"There's no visitors today, so you'll have to turn around and leave."

"Did you hear who his is, he's Reverend Jones." Moon replied back. "He presided over the funeral."

"I know who he is. Did you hear what I said? No visitors." The large man repeated then adjusted the position of the rifle toward the three.

"Now mister, we just wanted to be helpful, and you seem to be slightly misguided." Applebee stated as he pulled back his coat exposing his gun.

"I'll show you misguided." The man shouted back as he took a step forward.

Just has he made the move toward them, Mr. Sterling Price leaped from the buckboard and landed with all fours on the man's chest. He stumbled and fell backwards with Mr. Price attached to him. His large brim hat fell to the ground as his legs went out from under him and he landed on his back dropping the rifle. He pulled Mr. Price off him and reached for his rifle and started to point it at Mr. Price when Applebee quickly pulled his gun.

"I wouldn't do that if I was you." Applebee stated. "Drop the rifle and stand back." AJ jumped down and grabbed the rifle and place it in the buckboard. "Start walking in front of us." Applebee ordered as they continue toward the house.

As they stopped by the front porch of the house, Graham and Tomkins stepped out from inside, along with several other men.

"What's this all about? Graham asked.

"Well it seems your man here got slightly out of line. We thought we come by and see if there was anything we could do during this sad period." Applebee stated as he placed his gun back into his holster.

Graham and Tomkins looked at one another and then waved the other men to return to what they were doing.

"Why are you all dirty? Graham asked.

"I told them no visitor but that cat jumped me."

"What cat jumped you? He asked.

"The one in the back seat."

Graham looked and spotted the large yellow cat and waved his man to leave. He stepped back and faced Applebee.

"We want to be alone during this time. We don't need anything. Thanks for stopping by." Graham stated as he and Tomkins turned and started to return to the house.

"You know, this is the first time I've been out this way, mind if we take a quick ride around the land?

"Graham stopped and turned around. "I mind, just leave and let us be."

Applebee could hear the sound of several rifles cocking. The sound was coming from the sides of the house and from behind.

"Well, maybe another day." Applebee stated as they began to leave. The buckboard slowly turned around and exited out past the archway, down the entrance to the main road.

"Something going on." Applebee stated. "And we need to find out just what it is. I got a feeling that the mystery rider is somewhere on this ranch. When it gets dark, I think we'll make another visit."

"Some detective work. That's exciting. I read about this group called the Pinkerton detectives." AJ stated.

"The Pinkerton detectives, I've heard of them." Moon stated. "Remember Reverend Poke had that old newspaper that had that story about some detectives that were looking for some bad guy. Let's see, what was his name."

"You're not coming along. You and Mr. Price will stay behind." Applebee replied back. "If trouble breaks out I don't want you anywhere near it."

"If trouble breaks out you will need me to get you out of trouble." AJ stated.

"He's right Reverend. We might need someone if there becomes a problem. At least he can watch from a distance and get back to town." Moon replied.

"Let me think about it." Applebee stated. "Let's get back to town."

The wagon entered the outskirts of town passing by several of the businesses. Most were starting to close for the day. As they passed the bank, Applebee thought about his plans or lack of plans. He hadn't had much time to do any planning because of the church business kept interrupting his thoughts. Just then the buckboard stopped.

"Sheriff, what's up." Moon asked.

"What's that in the back seat? He asked

"That's our official rat killer that joined our little group." Moon replied.

"Rat killer." He stated back. "Good luck with that. I want you to me US Marshall Butte. He's down this way looking for someone."

Marshall Butte was an older man who stood tall and lean. His face was tanned and wrinkled from the sun and his clothes were dusty from traveling, but his badge was shiny. He stepped forward and handed Moon a wanted poster.

"Have any of you see this man? He asked.

Applebee's heart stopped beating for several seconds. He hadn't seen a wanted poster of him in some time. He looked over at the picture. It was a poor picture. Its features could have been most anyone.

"No sir, can't say I have." Moon replied.

"How about you Reverend," The Marshall asked.

"No, sorry." Applebee stated. "Why you looking for him"

"He tried to rob a bank in Texas and the information I got is that he came this way and may have passed through here." The Marshall replied as he stared at Applebee. "Haven't I seen you somewhere before? He asked. "You look a little familiar."

"I doubt that Marshall. You go to church much? Applebee replied back.

The Marshall stumbled for word for a second. "Church, no sir, moving around like I do doesn't give me much time for church. I guess I just have to keep looking." The Marshall stated as they handed him the poster. He folded the wanted poster and placed it in his coat pocket. "Thanks for your time."

"Let's go." Applebee stated as he watched with concern as the Marshall walked back to his horse. As the buckboard move on Applebee thought about his time in Texas but couldn't remember where in Texas and what happened there.

They reached the church building and parked the buckboard near the stable entrance. Sterling Price jumped down and darted inside the stable.

"Let's get some food in us, get the animals watered and fed." Applebee stated.

"I'll take care of the animals." AJ replied as he jumped down from the buckboard and hurried inside the stable. Suddenly a loud honking sound came from inside the stable.

"What's that sound? Applebee asked, as he and Moon started to enter the building. "It's coming from inside the stable."

AJ darted out carrying a small note. "Here." He stated as he handed the paper to Moon and then returned to the stable.

"What does it say? Applebee asked as he started to lean over Moon's should to read it.

"It says here that we are now the proud owners of one male goose. Donated by the Perce family." Moon stated as he handed Applebee the note.

"A goose. What are we going to do with a goose? Applebee stated as he looked up as the large gray goose came out of the stable area, it's wings fully spread, honking, with AJ in a full run.

It was a fully grown male goose. Gray in color with white on the tips of its wings. It stood with its wings fully spread, reaching at least a six-foot span. And he appeared to be in charge. Honking and waving his wings back and forth, the dust clouded and swirled around.

"We're turning into a farm." Applebee stated. "What we going to do with this guy?

"I had a goose when I was little. They ate bugs and snails and kept the place clean." Moon stated.

"Well good, if you know how to handle him, you're in charge of him." Applebee stated as he waved his hands in the air, turned and walked into the church building.

The goose settled down and appeared to be friendly to Moon as he stood next to him. Moon stroked his long neck and talked calmly to him as AJ was cautious and remained a few feet away.

"He's okay now, come on over and pet, let see, he needs a name. What should we call him? Moon asked as AJ slowly, inch his way closer until he was standing next to Moon.

"I know. We will call him Mr. Lincoln." Moon stated. "That's a good name."

CHAPTER

7

THE EVENING CLOSED IN AS Moon prepared the buckboard for the ride out to the Crane ranch. The full moon would provide sufficient light.

They reached the outskirts of the Crane Ranch. Moon pulled the buckboard off the road and into the oak trees that lined the road.

"No one standing at the entrance." Moon stated as he peered behind one of the large oak trees. "Guess they figure no one would be out at night."

"Good," Applebee stated as he walked behind Moon and looked toward the ranch house. "Here's what we'll do. Let's move around the south side of the barn, come in from the back. If anyone is being held there we should be able to see him."

"What you want me to do? AJ asked.

"I want you to stay here. If we get into any trouble, I want you the high tail it out of here and get some help." Applebee explained. "Who's that."

"Who's what? AJ asked.

"I thought I saw something moving in the back of the buckboard." Applebee stated as he and Moon took a step toward the buckboard.

Suddenly from the back, Sterling Price jumped down and slowly moved toward them.

"What's he doing here? Moon asked.

"I guess he jumped into the luggage section in the back of the buckboard. I didn't know he was there." AJ replied.

"Well, were stuck with him now." Applebee stated. "You need to keep him here and make sure he doesn't go wondering off. If we need to make a quick exit, we won't have time to chase him down."

Mr. Sterling Price sat quickly looking up at the three, as Applebee shook his head.

"Maybe we should see if Mr. Lincoln is here." Moon stated.

"Who's Mr. Lincoln? Applebee asked.

"The Goose." Moon replied.

"You named the goose Mr. Lincoln? He asked.

"That was the first name that came to me." Moon replied back.

"Come on, let's go. Applebee stated as the two moved along the fence line until they reached the back of the barn. They stopped and looked back at AJ. AJ wave giving them the clear sign. They slowly moved around the back until they reached the opening. It was wide enough for them to see in. Moon peered through the opening with Applebee watching for any movement from the ranch house.

"You were right," Moon stated. "Look there, near the back wall at the last horse stable."

"I see him." Applebee stated. "He's tied up. There's no one watching him either. Anyway we can get in without going through the front?

"Let me see if any of these boards are loose enough." Moon stated, as he began pulling on the side boards of the barn trying to find a loose board.

Midway down the side of the barn he found a board that was loose enough to pull free. Moon slowly continued to pull on the board until it broke free. The opening was enough for the two to squeeze through.

"Let me check on AJ." Applebee stated, as he walked back to the corner to catch sight of AJ. He then walked back where Moon had pulled other board loose.

"He's waving his hand okay. Why are you pulling more boards loose? He asked

"You see the size of that guy. He's not going to fit through this opening. One more board will make a little easier for us." Moon replied as he laid the board down on the ground.

They slowly took turns squeezing through the opening and quickly moved to the last stall. There, tied to the chair was who they were looking for. Moon reached down and pulled the gag out of his mouth.

"Are you a Crane? Moon asked.

"I am." He replied. "Am I glad to see the two of you. These guys jumped me as I was coming into town. Brought me here."

"My name is Reverend Jones and this is Moon. We found your horse grazing and brought him into town. "Applebee explained as Moon began untying him from the chair he was sitting in.

"My horse ran off when they jumped me and I guess they panicked." He replied back. "My name is Charles Crane. My mother wrote that she was terrible ill and I came as fast as I could.

"Listen to me. Your mother passed away and we need to get out of here before they decide to check on you." Applebee stated.

Charles was a large man. Balding and short. Moon was right to remove more of the barn siding. Because of his size they would not have been able to squeeze him through the opening. They moved to the opening when suddenly a voice shouted out at them.

"Don't go any further," The voice shouted out as the three stood facing the opening. "Well, if it isn't the good preacher."

They turned to see the man who they faced at the entrance of the grounds early in the day. His face had several scratches on it from Mr. Sterling Price claws.

"Move back over to the stall where I can keep an eye on you. You don't have the mangy cat to help you now." He stated was he wave his rifle at the three.

"I wish we did now." Moon said in a low voice.

The three slowly moved toward the back stable as they were told. Applebee needed the right time to draw his gun but knew that would bring more of them. He needed something else, something to draw the man's attention away from them. Suddenly it happened. The large man looked down to see Mr. Sterling Price rubbing on his leg. Then the man dropped to the ground, landing face down in the dirt and straw. The rife landed to his side. There, standing behind the man was AJ. In his hand was one of the large boards that Moon had removed. Moon quickly ran over and grabbed the rifle and check the man.

"He's out like a light." Moon stated.

"Thought you might need some help." AJ stated.

"No time for discussion." Applebee stated, "let's get out of here. Drag this guy over there and tie him up. Stick that rag in his mouth so he can't yell out."

Moon pulled the man to the back stall and tied him up using the rope that was there. When he finished he grabbed the rag and stuck it in his mouth and started to leave then stopped. Picking up an empty pail, he placed it over the man's head.

"There you go." Moon stated as he hurried over and squeezed through the opening. They moved alongside the back of the barn. They quickly moved across the open area until they reached the trees and reached the buckboard. They climbed into the buckboard and started to leave.

"Wait," Shouted AJ as Mr. Sterling Price jumped in.

"Let's go." Applebee shouted as Moon sped the buckboard back on the main road heading for town. He looked back. "This is one time I'm glad Mr. Sterling Price was with us." He stated as the buckboard sped off.

They reached town as Moon stopped the buckboard in front of the Sheriff's Office. Applebee told everyone to remain while he went to talk to the Sheriff. He jumped down and walked into the office.

"Where's the Sheriff? Applebee asked the elderly deputy.

"The Sheriff took the US Marshall to Bowman Creek. He'll be back sometime tomorrow. Deputy Magee is sick. I think he ate something that didn't sit right with him. Is there something I can do for you?

"No, guess not." Applebee replied back as he left returning to the buckboard.

"What did the Sheriff say? Moon asked.

"Sheriff out of town. Won't be back till tomorrow and the others are either sick and to old. Let's go."

Moon directed the buckboard to the back of the church pulling up to the doors of the stable.

"Take care of the horse and meet us inside." Applebee instructed as AJ jumped down and started to unhitch the horse.

They entered the building as Moon placed some wood into the iron stove.

"Now that was a terrible experience." Charles stated. "What's going to happen now?

"Well, I figure they'll probably try to get you back without causing too much of a stir. What are they after? Applebee asked.

"There after the ranch and the cash my mother has in the bank. The lawyer has the paperwork that indicates Graham as the only living relative. When they found out I was coming they devised a plan to take me out. Tomorrow there supposed to go to the bank and complete the arrangements. I think they have a buyer for the ranch. Some man from back east."

"Well, we can stop that, providing we can get through tonight." Moon stated.

"We'll stay on our guard tonight and maybe we'll get lucky and they might decide to move on knowing that we know who they are and what there up to." Applebee stated.

"We can take turns watching." Applebee stated as he reached over and grabbed a tin cup and poured some coffee.

AJ guided the horse into the stable and as Mr. Lincoln quickly darted out the door. AJ tied the horse in the stall and placed the water bucket and grain inside the stall. He ran out to catch Mr. Lincoln but quickly gave up and returned to the church.

"Get the everything taken care of? Moon asked.

"Got everything taken care of except for Mr. Lincoln who decided to take a walk. I tried to catch him but he's too fast for me." AJ stated.

"Don't worry about him now." Applebee stated.

CHAPTER

8

S EVERAL HOURS HAD PASSED SINCE they arrived back and the night was busy as usual. The sound of the piano music from the saloon could be heard through the cool crisp night air.

Graham and Tomkins and several of his men rode into town stopping at the saloon. They gathered inside the saloon and had several drinks, talked, then left. They stopped across the street from the Church and slowly made their way around to the back of the Church locating themselves in different positions.

Inside Applebee and the rest were quietly sitting with Moon watching near the window.

"I think I see some movement." Moon stated.

"Where? Applebee asked as he jumped up and pulled his revolver and looked out the window."

"There by the edge of the building." Moon replied as he pointed to the building next to the Church.

"I sure hope you locked the front door of the building? Applebee asked.

"I thought I did." Moon replied back as they continued to peer out the window.

"Sorry gentlemen but the door was unlocked." Graham stated as he and Tomkins entered.

"Guess I didn't." Moon stated as they stepped back.

"Reverend you're a busy man. You stick your nose into all kinds of business. I heard talk about you." Graham stated.

Applebee was the last to turn around as he quickly placed his gun back under his coat and then raised his hands.

"Let's get this over with." Tomkins said as he grabbed Moons rifle and laid it aside and then opened the back door. "What do you say we take a walk out to the stable?

"Let's go, move." Graham ordered as they moved from the building to outside, then to inside the stable.

The Lantern was still lit when they entered the stable. Graham waved his gun directing them to the back wall. He instructed the other men to remain outside and watch the street.

"Well, it was nice knowing you, but we have business to take care of in the morning and I'm afraid you're in our way."

Suddenly a loud screeching sound could be heard as Mr. Lincoln darted out from the entrance past the others. His wings spread and his Talen's lifted high in the air striking Graham in his chest cutting into his shirt. Applebee quickly pulled his revolver and fired hitting Tomkins and then firing again knocking Graham to the ground. Moon quickly grabbed Grahams and Tomkins revolver and ran to the door. The other men saw what had happened, ran to their horses and hurried out of town.

"AJ run and get the deputy." Applebee stated as he held his gun on the two as Moon grabbed some rope and tied their hands.

The two moaned from their wounds as they laid on the floor of the stable.

AJ returned with the elderly deputy along with several other people who heard the shooting.

"You need to take these two, maybe even treat their wounds. Moon and Mr. Crane here will go with you and explain." Applebee stated.

The deputy and the others removed the two and marched them to the Sheriff's Office with Moon and Mr. Crane following. A larger crowd had gathered and watched.

"I guess I got to thank Mr. Lincoln for saving our lives." Applebee stated.

"Do we need to vote Mr. Lincoln into the family? AJ asked.

"No, we'll skip the formality." Applebee replied back as they left the stable.

"Can he come inside? AJ asked.

"The building? Applebee replied back. "You know what kind of a mess this guy will make? "I guess."

Leroy Dobbs wrote down the last of the information and then leaned back. "My hand is tired, but I got it all."

"So what happened after that? Did you ever get the chance to make your plans on the bank? Dobbs asked.

Applebee rolled his wheelchair around and faced the window. "Another day maybe, I'm very tired."

"Okay, me too. I need to get this story off. I'd like to come by in a couple of days and get more of the story." Dobbs stated.

Applebee just nodded and stared out the window. Dobbs said his goodbyes and hurried out the door making sure the door didn't slam shut. He quickly moved along the street making his way across main street to the hotel. He hurried up the stairs entering his room

Several hours had passed. He made his way to the telegraph office and sent a message to his editor, then returned to the hotel for dinner. He sat quietly, ordered his dinner and afterwards returned to his room.

The sounds of the busy street below slowly became quiet again as the sounds of the saloons, the laughter, and terrible singing came alive as it did each night. He laid thinking about the story he just gathered and how it must have been during those years until sleep overwhelmed him.

CHAPTER

9

TWO DAYS HAD PASSED SINCE he last met with Applebee and Dobbs was eager to get another chapter in the life of Applebee Jones written down. He dressed, grabbed a cup of coffee from the diner and hurried across main street to Miss Millie's Boarding House. He knocked on the screen door but there was no answer. He opened the door slightly.

"Hello, Miss Millie. It's me Leroy Dobbs."

He could hear her in the distance coming closer from the back of the house. "Hello Mr. Dobbs, I was in the back. Please come in." She said.

"I wanted to meet with the Reverend again today." He stated.

"You don't know do you? She stated in a very somber voice. The Reverend passed away in his sleep two days ago. I'm so sorry. It was so busy around here I just forgot to get in touch with you."

"He died? Dobbs replied.

"Yes, his body is at the Fry's Funeral Home. I telegraphed his son the day he passed. He should be arriving sometime today."

"His son. I wasn't aware that he had a son." Dobbs stated in surprise.

"Yes, that's who pay for his stay here all this time." Miss Millie replied back.

"Thank you," he shouted out as he hurried out the door as it slammed shut. He once again yelled out, "Sorry."

Back along the street he stopped a man reading a paper and asked him the direction to Fry's Funeral home. The man pointed to the end of the street and Dobbs made his way through the increasing traffic to the funeral home.

It was a decorative building with lots of thick red and purple curtains. Entering he was met by a man who introduced himself as Mr.

Fry. He was tall and thin, with plenty of dark hair that was parted down the middle using an abundance of hair grease.

"Can I help you? He asked.

"You have Applebee Jones here? Dobbs asked.

"Yes sir, and it is the Reverend Applebee Jones. Are your family? He asked.

"Kind of." Dobbs replied.

"The funeral will be on Friday at 11 am at the Bakers Ridge Cemetery. Will you be joining us? Fry asked.

"Yes, I'll be there." Dobbs replied, turned and left. He hurried over to the telegraph office and sent a telegram to his editor about the death of Applebee and that he would be staying for the funeral and then returning.

As he walked back to the hotel he thought about how he was going to end the story. He hadn't put any thought into it but now he had to make the story complete needing to finish it somehow.

He stopped along the way and found a bench to sit on and stared out into the street. The town busy with people moving about. Several freight wagons rolled through town stacked high with wooden crates. The town Marshall walked by tipping his hat to those he passed. The sound of the Train could be heard in the distance. The billowing clouds of black smoke could be seen lifting up into the sky above the buildings.

Large crowds began to gather at the station as the train pulled in with its screeching brakes and its loud blast of steam as it came to a halt. Dobbs could see large groups of passengers getting off and then many getting on. Baggage was scattered on the wooden station platform. He watched as two men walked along the street to the Hotel his was staying at and entered. His first thought was they were just travelers. Then thought maybe they could be here for the funeral. Miss Millie said they would be arriving today. He jumped up from the bench, crossed the busy street to the hotel and walked in. The two men were standing at the counter. He walked up to the counter and stood close trying to listen to the conversation.

"Thank you Mr. Hick. Your room will be up the stairs and the second door to the left and yours will be the next room. Do you need any assistance? The clerk asked.

"No we'll be fine." The older man stated.

"Excuse me gentlemen, but would either of you be here for the funeral of Applebee Jones? Dobbs asked.

The two men looked at one another, "Yes we both are. Is there something you need? The younger name asked.

"You don't know me. My name is Leroy Dobbs. I am a journalist from San Francisco." Dobbs stated as he reached his hand out.

"Well Mr. Dobbs what can we do for you? The older one replied back.

"Which of you would be Burton Hicks son? Dobbs asked.

There was silence at first, then the older man spoke. "I'm James Hicks, Burton Hicks was my father. This is AJ."

"I thought I recognized you. Some time ago I heard you speak about a man you were raised by. I followed that story and all the leads there were to this town, where your father had settled down at a boarding house."

"An why would you do that? Hicks asked.

"Because the story was so intriguing that we wanted to make a full feature of it. Can we sit for a few minutes? Dobbs asked as they agreed and moved to the diner and sat.

"I've travel for months following leads from state to state. I was about to give up when the train stopped here and I got off to take a train break. I found your father by chance and I've been here with your father all week. He's been providing me the details of his life. I went back today, we were going to continue on and I just found out that he passed away. I am so sorry for your loss." Dobbs stated.

"My father retired here after a long time of ministering. He just didn't want to leave. I've been paying for his stay Miss Millie's Boarding House all this time. The church provides some funds. But you know, we have traveled a long distance and we need to get to our rooms. Can we continue this another time? Hicks asked. "And I can imagine you have several questions you want to ask AJ."

"Yes I do. Can we meet after the funeral? Dobbs asked.

"Of course. AJ will be presiding over the funeral."

Dobbs reached out and shook their hands and watched them leave the dining room. He now had an ending to his story. The funeral was days away and that would bring the story of Applebee Jones to a close. But there was still one last thing he wanted to do.

He left the Hotel and made his way through the street until he reached the church. He stopped and examined the building and the coral that was located near the back. He walked to the back toward the stable. He leaned on the corral rail watching the one horse move about. He thought about Applebee's horse Donk and the stories he told of how Donk escaped from the coral. It drew a smile on his face. From behind him he heard a voice.

"Can I help you? The voice asked.

Dobbs turned around and saw a man walking toward him. He was dressed in old working clothes. Faded pants, a worn out shirt and straw hat.

"I was just looking. I'm Leroy Dobbs from San Francisco. I'm here for the funeral of Reverend Jones. I just wanted to see where he worked." Dobbs stated.

"Good old Reverend Jones. He's been around for some time now. Too bad about his passing. He was well into his 90's. Lived a long time. I'm Henry Watson. I'm the care taker of this place." Watson stated as he walked over and leaned on the railing looking into the corral.

"Who the Pastor of the Church now? Dobbs asked.

"That would be Reverend Henry P. Pocket." Watson replied back. "He's been here for some time. But there's been several Pastors who were here after Reverend Jones. The place hasn't change much either."

"Want to walk around? Watson asked. "I knew Old Moon. I was just a kid at the time. But, I remember him with Reverend Jones and another kid at the time."

They walked toward the barn as Dobb's looked inside. The building was run down and many of the shingles were missing in the roof. Is the chicken coop still in the back? Dobbs asked.

"The coop is there but no chickens." He replied back. "It's getting worn down. There's a room off to the side where Moon and the kid used to live. At least that what I was told. It's a storage room now for junk."

"The Reverend Pocket should be back soon. You want to wait around for him? He asked.

"No that's okay. I just wanted to see the place. I need to get back." Dobbs stated.

He took one last look and left. He made his way along the street passing the businesses until he reached the other end of town. He wanted to see what Swayne's store looked like. The place had changed owners several times during all the years. He stopped short as he reached the location. He had remembered the story of the Connelly brothers and the events that took place. The store now had a different sign hanging in the front. Miles Furniture Store was painted in big black letters with several different pieces of furniture displayed near the doorway and along the side.

"Is there anything I can help you with sir? A man stated.

"No sir," Dobbs stated back. "I just remembered when this was Swayne's place."

"Swayne's, seem like I remember someone saying that name. That had to have been a long time ago. This building has been many things since those days." The man stated. "Sure I can't interest you in some hand crafted furniture?

"No thanks." Dobbs replied back as he turned and started walking back to the Hotel.

He reached the Hotel, entered walking past the clerk's counter. He climbed the stairs to his room. Walked over to the French doors and opened them to allow the air to flow through the room.

10

THE FUNERAL

THE DAY OF THE FUNERAL was now here. Dobbs hurried down the stairs and walked to the funeral home. Several others were walking in as he arrived. He was greeted by Fry as he entered and then by James Hicks and AJ. He walked to the back and found a chair in the back. Miss Millie waved to him as she sat up front.

A hand full of people were there for the service. Dobbs thought about Applebee's age being in the mid 90's, most of those who lived through those days were probably dead by now

AJ walked to the front standing behind the closed coffin. "I want to thank you for coming this day as we lay to rest a man who came to this town so long ago, and helped make it the town that it is today. He was a different kind of man, a pastor with strength, not afraid to face the evils that lurked here in those days. He was awarded with a long life. Most of those who knew him are now gone as well. I grew up with Reverend Applebee Jones. Myself and Moon, who passed away several years ago. Mr. Sterling Price, the cat and who could forget Mr. Lincoln the goose that was given to us. I will never forget all the hard times we faced together and all of the laughter we had together. I would like to introduce the son of Applebee Jones who would like to say a few words."

James Hicks walked to the front and stood before the gathering. "I also want to thank all of you for coming. I know my father held this town close to his heart. When I came to see him I offered him a place with me and my family but here is where he wanted to be and here is where he stayed even to this day. If you like to join us at the cemetery now we will complete today's service."

Dobbs followed the group through the street and the short distance to the cemetery. As they gathered around the men placed the coffin on the supports. AJ stepped forward and began to speak.

"I once watched Reverend Jones preside over a funeral where he knocked over the casket. It was a moment that shook the entire congregation. But the Reverend handled it with class. He looked down at the body and then to those watching and said. Did you feel the ground shake? He had his ways but in all of those awkward moments when we needed someone to step forward he was the one who did it. Now we say our goodbyes. Please, let's take a few moments in silence."

The service ended and the entire group began the walk back to town. Dobbs walked with Miss Millie until they reached the church then she said her goodbyes and went back to her boarding house.

Dobbs returned to the Hotel along with James Hicks and AJ. They stopped in at the bar for a beer and then sat in the parlor.

"I would like to know where you came into the picture? Dobbs asked James Hicks. "Applebee never mentioned you at all."

"Let me take back to the beginning. My father and mother where married very young. When I was born they decided to move west like many others. We joined a wagon train that was moving in that direction. Somewhere in the mid-west the wagon train was attacked my Indians. My father fought bravely but was seriously injured. The wagon train was over taken. My mother and myself were taken away along many others who were enslaved for some time. My mother worked the fields for such a long time and was wore down by the forced labor. When my father recovered from his wounds, he vowed to find us and spent years looking for us. But the tribe we were with continued to move around. We were finally attacked by the US Army. They stormed into the camp and killed everyone in sight. My mother and I, along with other women and children hid in the fields until it was over. They burned everything in sight. Those that survived moved on to newer camps. One day a family who had a ministry came by and noticed us and took us in. They moved around a lot, but we were safe. My father eventually located the tribe that was destroyed by the Army, but we were long gone by then.

He spent years searching for us, but never did located us. He ran out of money and I guess had to choose a different way of life. Later on in years I heard a story about a man who lost his family to the Indian raids and I went searching for him. I was an adult by then and had my own family. Mother had died from disease. I think she was just worn out. I finally found him. We met and we kept close contact with one another since. When he came here to Bakers Ridge, I would check on him from time to time. He would write. He used to talk about AJ and Moon a lot. He would even write about old Donk. When he got old he didn't want to leave, so I paid for him to stay at Miss Millie's boarding house."

"And what about you AJ." Dobbs asked as he continued to take notes.

"I don't know what he told you, but I can tell you this, he sure wasn't afraid of anything or anybody. I always wondered about him carrying a gun. He was so different. At times I didn't think he had any religious training at all. But he changed the lives of many people. For me, he wanted me to be educated. He saved up enough money to send me to school. At first I didn't want to leave him or Moon, but he insisted. I would come back to see them both at least twice a year. I remember he used to go and sit each day on a bench in town across from the Bank and watch the people come and go. He knew the movement, time and all the details of the Bank. He was there every day. I don't think we ever found out why he did it. Sometimes Mr. Sterling Price or Mr. Lincoln would follow him and sit next to him. The towns people used to laugh when they saw him sitting there with one or the other next to him. But he didn't care and no one would question him. When Mr. Lincoln would start making a racket he would take out his gun and tell the goose if he wanted to be a part of Christmas dinner. Mr. Lincoln would shut right up. They became so attached to one another. Once in church, during the service, Mr. Lincoln came in through the open front doors, marched right down the center of the building during service with his wings all spread out making all kinds of noise. When he got to the front the Reverend took out his gun and pointed it at him. The Reverend would say, well if it isn't our Christmas goose. Mr. Lincoln would turn around and almost fly out of the building. The entire congregation would break out in laughter. It would take some time for everyone to calm themselves down."

"So what happened? Dobbs asked.

"Well, everything seems to come to an end. Mr. Sterling Price got so big from eating Moon's biscuits and gravy that he could hardly walk. He would lay around most of the day. He forgot about any rats. Then it happened. On day, a large male coyote got into the chicken coup and started killing the chickens. Mr. Sterling Price saw it and jumped on the back of that coyote and rode him like a bull rider but the coyote was much too big and he killed Mr. Price and Reverend killed the coyote. I think the death of Mr. Sterling Price broke the Reverend Jones heart. Then several months later Donk died in the stable. He just got so old and had a hard time moving. You know, Reverend would sit for hours talking to the Donk, the cat, and the goose. It was like they knew what he was saying. Moon and I used to think he had some animal connection, it was sure strange. He used to take the buckboard out at least once a week for a ride down to the river where we used to go fishing. We'd all load up, including you know who, and he would just sit near a shady oak tree. Moon and I would fish and the Reverend would enjoy the scenery. Mr. Price and Mr. Lincoln would steal the bait, even grab a fish we caught and we'd have to chase after them. Reverend would just laugh. Mr. Lincoln died one day. He was just old too, lived out his time I guess. Reverend Jones had them all buried behind the barn next to one of the old oak trees. He would visit them at least once a week."

"So what happened to Moon. You said he died several years ago." Dobbs asked.

"You two want another beer? Hicks asked as both nodded.

"This young couple had arranged with me to get married in the church on a Saturday morning. Reverend Jones was in front of them reading what I had written for him. When he got to the part about, if anyone has an objection to these to getting hitched keep it to yourself. He loved to say that. Suddenly a young man in the very back of the church jumped up and yelled out "I do. That's my girl and he stole her from me." The Reverend yelled back, didn't you hear what I said? The man ran forward shouting and waving his hands. The groom and the man began arguing and soon fists were flying. The bride was a large gal.

She joined in using the flowers as a weapon and when those were gone she started throwing punches. The Reverend just watched for several seconds and then walked over and sat down. Moon hurried over to the Reverend and asked about breaking it up. The Reverend said: the last two standing will be the ones who will marry.

"What happened? Dobbs asked as Hicks handed each one a beer.

"Well they rolled around for a while and then everyone got tired and stopped." AJ explained.

"Who was left standing? Dobbs asked.

"The groom and the young man. The bride took a punch and was out cold. Moon told the Reverend that this was not going to be a good marriage."

"Did he finish the ceremony? Dobbs asked.

"No. It took both of them to carried her out and everyone disappeared. Never heard from them again. Reverend Jones told Me not to schedule anymore weddings on Saturday.

"Did he continue to carry a gun? Dobbs asked. "I know when I went to see him he had one under the blanket."

"He never went anywhere without it." AJ stated. "Everyone thought he was fast with a gun, but really, he was just accurate in using it. He used it on a few heads many a time."

"I know, he told the story about the Connelly's who bullied the town for some time." Dobbs stated.

"The older he got, the gun was more of a show piece. His vision got bad and he was aware of it." AJ replied back

"What happened to Moon? Dobbs asked.

"Moon started getting sick. The Reverend wrote me and told me the Doc in town through he had a cancer. So when I came down to visit I took Moon back with me to see a specialist. The Reverend gave me all the money he had so that I could pay for it. He told me to bring Moon back when he was well."

"Did he ever get better? Dobbs asked.

"No, he gradually got worse, But, he lived a long time, lived into his 90's. Then one day he told me he needed to see the Reverend but that never happened. He died several days later." AJ stated. "I sent a telegraph to Miss Millie asking her to inform the Reverend of Moon's death."

"I think my father felt the loss of those he loved hard. He came to his town alone. Found companionship, joy, friendship and then ended up alone again." Hicks stated as he finished his beer.

"In all the things he told you, did he ever say anything about why he sat in front of the bank every day? AJ asked. "Did he just like to watch people?

"I'd like to know why he took the name of Applebee Jones. He never spoke about it. When I asked him he said it was important or he just changed the subject. I took that as he didn't want to talk about it. So I left it alone." Hicks explained.

Dobbs thought for a second knowing that he knew the real facts and he thought Hicks might know something as well of the story about the bank. "I will tell you this. Read my story when it comes out and you decide. And you Mr. Hicks will learn how he took the name of Applebee Jones."

They agreed the day was over and they needed to catch the train back the next day. Dobbs folded his notes and they made their way to their rooms.

Dobbs tossed everything on the bed and went to the window. He looked out and watched the movement of the City as the day was coming to a close and the early evening was beginning to take shape. Suddenly there was a knock at his door. He moved to the door and opened it and saw Miss Millie standing in the entrance.

"Miss Millie, is everything alright? He asked. "Please come in."

Miss Millie entered the room and turned and handed Dobbs a box, the size of a shoe box

.

"I was clearing out Reverend Jones room and I found this box. It had a note in it. She stated. "I need to get back, I have a new house guest and he's a little fussy. Open it, it's addressed to you."

Miss Millie left as Dobbs opened the box. Inside was an object that was wrapped in a cloth with a note sitting on top. He walked over to the edge of the bed and sat down, taking the note out. He opened it and read the note. The writing was difficult to read. The words were misspelled and were uneven in the sentences, but he was able to make out the meaning.

"I want you to have this. I have had this here pistol all of my days. It hasn't fired a bullet in 35 years. It is a part of my story. Please take care of it."

Dobbs read the letter and folded it, placing it back into the box, then replacing the lid on the box. He thought to himself that Applebee knew his time had come. He appreciated and was honored with the fact that he left his treasured prize with him to care for. He placed the box on the bed and removed his shoes and coat. He stretched out looking up at the ceiling until the thoughts of the day slowly faded away and sleep came upon him.

CHAPTER

11

MORNING ARRIVED WITH THE SOUNDS of the street below. The window of the room was left open and a breeze blew in along with the shouting and the rolling wagons. A gas driven vehicle sputtered by adding to the sound of a new day. Dobbs looked at the clock on the wall which struck 9 o'clock. He jumped up, got dressed, gathered his things and made his way down the stairs and entered the dining room.

"What would you like? The young waitress asked.

"Where is......." he started to ask but was interrupted.

"She doesn't work today. You got me this morning." She replied back. "Would you like some coffee?

"Yes, and you know what, I'd like a chunk of apple pie." Dobbs stated as he placed his hat on the table.

"A chunk of apple pie. You mean a slice of apple pie? She replied back.

Dobbs smiled and looked up at the young girl, "a slice of apple pie, no, a chunk of apple pie."

"You better not have any spurs on, our chairs are getting scratched up." She stated as she turned and left for the kitchen.

"I don't wear spurs," he shouted back watching her leave.

Dobbs sat quietly sipping his coffee and taking bites of the apple pie. He would peer out the window at times and watch the movement on the street.

"Can I join you? James Hicks asked as he walked up to the table. "Hope you don't mind some company?

"No, please sit." Dobbs replied back.

"The train leaves in an hour and I thought I'd wait here rather than sit on the bench at the station." He stated as the young girl brought another cup of coffee.

"You're not wearing any spurs are you? She asked. "Our chairs are getting scratched up by those spurs."

"What, spurs? Hicks replied back. "I don't wear spurs."

"Are you heading back today? He asked.

"Yes, there's nothing more to learn here." Dobbs replied.

"You got your story? Hicks asked.

"Yeah, I got the story." Dobbs replied. "I'm glad you came and I had the opportunity to meet you or I wouldn't have been able to complete the story."

"Gentlemen, is there room for one more? AJ stated, as he walked over. "Are we all leaving today? He asked.

"Yep, I'm taking the train home today." Dobbs stated.

AJ reached over and grabbed a chair from another table, pulled it over and sat. He looked back at the waitress and waved his hand indicating he needed a cup as well.

"I'd like to know who took over for Applebee when he retired? Dobbs asked as he continue to eat.

"Well, let see. There were many who came and left. None were like Applebee. He was one of a kind. I was gone through that period so I don't know who they were."

They sat and talked for the good part of an hour and then they left for the train station. A large crowd had gathered. Reaching the station, they could hear the sound in the distance of the locomotive. They could see the large pillowing clouds of smoke lifting into the air in the distance above the rolling hills. The large crowd began to ready themselves as the train rounded the last hill and was now visible. As it drew closer families and friends said their goodbyes. There luggage stacked on carts. The train slowly moved past the crowd and stopped with a bellow of steam blasting out of the locomotive. Several people stepped down from the cars and tried to move through the crowd as the crowd began climbing the steps to the different cars.

Dobbs, Hicks and AJ found seats in the second car facing each other. The trip home would take another full day and each would get off at different stops along the way.

"Well, you got your story now, so what happens with it?" AJ asked as he took off his coat and toss it above in the over- head carrier

"It will be a story that will run in the paper I'm sure, but I know that a book will be published. It should make great reading." Dobbs stated as he looked out the side window. The train slowly began to move, inching its way past the station dock until it began to pick up speed. Black smoke clouded the sky above.

"I'd like to get one of those books." Hicks stated. The story of my father's life needs to be pasted on to our future families."

"I'll make sure you get a copy of the story." Dobbs stated.

"Don't forget me." AJ replied. "If it wasn't for Applebee I probably wouldn't be here today."

"Your both on my list." Dobbs remarked back.

"So what's next for you? Hicks asked. "Take on another assignment somewhere.?

"I hear a story about a thing called a lightbulb that generates a bright light. Bright enough to see at night. You can bet they will have something for me to follow up on." Dobbs replied. "You know; I'd like to learn more about who the real Applebee Jones really was. What happened to him. He was never found, just his suit cases. I wonder where he disappeared to?

"That might make a great story," AJ replied back.

THE END

Printed in the United States
By Bookmasters